My Cat Macaroni

by Geoff Patton
illustrated by David Clarke

RISING

the school

Sam's house

the
supermarket

SUPERMARKET

2

to Emily's house

to Lin's apartment

Con's house

3

me
(Sam)

Grandpa

Hi. My name is Sam.

This is my family.

Chapter 1
Can I Have a Cat?

I asked Dad, 'Dad, can I have a cat?'
'No, Sam,' said Dad.

I said to Dad, 'If I can have a cat,
I will clean my room every Monday.'
'No, Sam,' said Dad.

I said, '**Please**, **please**, **please**,
can I have a cat?'
'**No**, **no**, **no**,' said Dad.

Dad can ask me to clean my room,
but he can't make me do it.

Chapter 2
Go and Ask Mum

I asked Mum, 'Mum, can I have a cat?'
'No, Sam,' said Mum.

I said to Mum, 'If I can have a cat,
I will play with Susie every Tuesday.'
'No, Sam,' said Mum.

I said, '**Please**, **please**, **please**,
can I have a cat?'
'**No**, **no**, **no**,' said Mum.

Mum can ask me to play with Susie,
but she can't make me do it.

KK292608

Chapter 3
Will Gran Let Me?

I asked Gran, 'Gran, can I have a cat?'
'No, Sam,' said Gran.

I said to Gran, 'If I can have a cat, I will
do judo with you every Wednesday.'
'No, Sam,' said Gran.

I said, '**Please**, **please**, **please**,
can I have a cat?'
'**No**, **no**, **no**,' said Gran.

13

Gran can ask me to do judo, but she can't make me do it.

Chapter 4
What about Grandpa?

I asked Grandpa, 'Grandpa,
can I have a cat?'
'Yes, Sam,' said Grandpa.

I said, 'If I can have a cat, I will
let you tell me stories about the
olden days every Thursday.'
'Yes, Sam,' said Grandpa.

I said, '**Please**, **please**, **please**,
can I have a cat?'
'**Yes**, **yes**, **yes**,' said Grandpa.

Grandpa said, 'Yes!'
That's how Macaroni came into
our family.

Chapter 5
My Cat Macaroni

This is Macaroni.

He is my cat. He watches me a lot.

On Monday he watches me clean
my room.

On Tuesday he watches me play
with Susie.

On Wednesday he watches me do
judo with Gran.

On Thursday he watches me while
Grandpa tells me stories. But ...

... on Friday, Saturday and Sunday,
he is all mine.

Well, most of the time.

Survival Tips

Tips for getting a cat when everyone says no

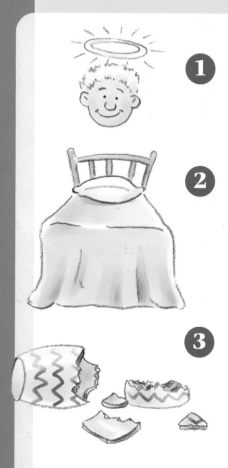

1 Be really good. If you are really good you might get your way.

2 Make your bed every day. It has nothing to do with cats, but it might make your dad happy. That can't be bad.

3 Ask for a cat when your mum and dad are in a good mood. When you have just broken your mum's best vase is not a good time.

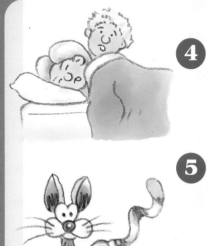

4 Keep asking — you might get Mum at a weak moment.

5 Look after your best friend's kitten, just for one night. You may decide you don't want one.

Riddles and Jokes

Sam Ten cats were on a ship. One jumped off. How many were left?

Con None because they were all copycats.

Con When is it bad luck to see a black cat?

Sam When you are a mouse.

Sam What did the cat say when he fell off the boat?

Con Nothing. Cats can't talk.